MORE ADVANCE PRAISE

In The Wake Of Suicide may be "A Child's Journey", but it can be of exceptional benefit for anyone seeking to understand and accept a terrible event in their lives. It's a great tool for a parent experiencing grief and having to "try" and help their child get through a tragedy.

God Bless Mrs. Kaulen for simplifying such difficult circumstances! She takes the pain of a child and demonstrates vividly how "We can do all things through Christ who strengthens us!"

John Baxter, LCDC, NCACH, CFBCC
(in other words, a learned Christian Counselor)

This book represents a sincere and realistic explanation of a child's reaction to a parent's suicide. The journey from depression to the actual loss of the father and then the young man's ability to cope with these tragic events is presented beautifully from a Christian and Biblical point of view.

Julian S. Haber, Pediatrician and Author

The death of a parent by suicide is a tough issue for a child to deal with. It is especially hard to help them understand how God still loves them and their parent who committed suicide. This book helped my children deal with the fact that their father, who committed suicide, is still loved by God. It helped them understand that God can help them through ANY tragedy that they may face in their lives. Not only did it help them--it helped me answer questions about suicide and religion. This book is a wonderful tool to encourage communication about suicide and God.

Laura Somwaru
Mother of 3 children whose father committed suicide

Through the eyes of young Max, the reader witnesses the unmanageable and overwhelming pain and confusion of parental suicide. A taboo topic that affects far too many people, suicide and its repercussions are seldom addressed as honestly, kindly and graciously as is accomplished in this small book.

In spite of the sorrow, guilt and anger, the healing Voice of a tender, merciful and loving God speaks into this darkest night of human experience. In the Wake of Suicide is a must-read, not only for children trying to cope with the reality, but for anyone who has suffered through the doubts, questions, rage and hurt, as well as for those who provide care and support following a suicide.

(the Rev.) Elizabeth Moreau
United Methodist minister, Texas Annual Conference

IN THE WAKE OF SUICIDE
A Child's Journey

By Diane Bouman Kaulen, MS, CCLS

Illustrations by Grami & O'Pa McAdoo

LONGHORN CREEK PRESS

If interested in donating to make copies of this book available free to families with limited funds, or if you would like to receive such a copy, please go to www.InTheWakeOfSuicide.com

First Edition

Cover Art and Illustrations by Grami and O'Pa McAdoo
www.RiverBottomRanch.com

ISBN 978-0-9764026-5-7

Library of Congress Cataloging-in-Publication Data

Kaulen, Diane Bouman.
 In the wake of suicide : a child's journey / Diane Bouman Kaulen ; [illustrations by Grami and O'Pa McAdoo]. -- 1st ed.
    p. cm.
 Summary: After struggling with feelings of anger, grief, and guilt, Max learns to rely on God's strength and his family's Christian faith while coping with his father's suicide.
 ISBN 978-0-9764026-5-7 (alk. paper)
 [1. Suicide--Fiction. 2. Fathers and sons--Fiction. 3. Grief--Fiction. 4. Christian life--Fiction.] I. McAdoo, Grami, ill. II. McAdoo, O'Pa, ill. III. Title.
 PZ7.K1712In 2008
 [E]--dc22
                              2007035898

Inquiries for volume purchases of this book may be directed to Longhorn Creek Press.

To request author for speaking engagement or autographed copies, contact Sales@LonghornCreekPress.com.

Please visit www.LonghornCreekPress.com
And
www.InTheWakeOfSuicide.com

Author's Dedication

To Jacob, Ethan and Isaiah
May God's love comfort you.

Hi. My name is Max, and here's my dad. I like being with him. We enjoy playing games like checkers and monopoly.

The best is when he reads me books; he gets really into the stories. Sometimes, we just hang out and watch TV together. I love my dad. Well, most of the time.

Lately, my dad sleeps a lot, usually almost the whole time he's home. Mom says he sleeps way too much. My parents yell everyday about him always sleeping and not spending more time with all of us.

I think he must be sick because he walks and talks funny when he finally is awake. We don't play games that much anymore, and he rarely comes to watch me play baseball.

It seems like he's always mad at me these days. When I try to talk to him, he tells me to get away and leave him alone. If I make too much noise, he yells for me to go to my room.

My dad takes lots of medicine, but it doesn't seem to help. I don't know why it doesn't make him better. He drinks a lot of alcohol, too. Lots of nights, I fall asleep listening to Mom and Dad hollering at each other.

Then I wake up in the middle of the night and find my dad asleep in strange places. Mom will usually be in their bed crying. I feel so bad about it. A lot of the time I go back to my bed and cry, but nobody knows.

My dad must be getting sicker. He always goes to the doctors, and I don't understand why they don't make him better. Mom says in order for him to get well, he has to leave our house.

I don't understand. If he is sick, doesn't he need us to help him even more? And if he isn't home with us, who will check to see that he doesn't take too much medicine or make sure he even wakes up everyday?

It does seem a little quieter at my house, but I sure miss him.

My dad lives somewhere else now. He's getting sicker and sicker, and I see him less and less. I tell him that if he gets better and comes home, I will never be loud again. He's still not better though, and he isn't coming home either.

My mom tells my little brothers and me that Dad is sick with an illness called depression. It makes him do things that he normally wouldn't do. She has to keep us safe. She says Dad can come home if he makes the right choices and works with the doctors. She says it's up to him; he has to decide.

Why won't he choose to get better? Doesn't he love me? Doesn't he want to be with us?

Then the worst day of my life happened.
When I got home from school, my house was
full of people. My grandparents, the pastor at
our church, and some people I didn't even
know were all there.

I could tell my mom had been crying. She told me that my dad's depression had got worse. His mind
was so sick that he couldn't think right. Because of the depression, my dad died.

He was dead. I was so sad. I wanted to cry, but I didn't. I couldn't.

Later on, I found out that my dad wanted to die. In fact, he made himself die. They called his death a
suicide. What? My dad wanted to die?"

I was so mad. I wanted to yell.

I was mad at my mom for not doing things to make him better.

I was mad at my dad for leaving me.

I was mad at myself for doing all those things that made my dad mad.

I was mad that all my friends' dads were happy, and mine never was.

I was mad that my brothers always got in my way.

I was mad I always have to keep my room clean.

I was mad that my dad did not love me enough to want to live.

I was mad that I would never see my dad again.

And I was mad at God.

Why, God? Why did you let my dad die? Why didn't you save him?

I wanted my dad back! I wanted him happy! I wanted him to love me enough to stay alive. I couldn't believe I would never see him again.

He would never come home. He was dead.

My stomach felt sick. My whole body felt numb. I couldn't breathe or swallow. Everyone kept coming around to be with me, but I just wanted to be left alone.

After Dad died, everything changed. We moved out of our house so I didn't live by my friends anymore.

I got into trouble all the time. If I screamed at my mom, she grounded me. If I hit my brother, she sent me to my room. And if I didn't look happy every minute, my mom cried. Everyone expected me to talk about my feelings and I didn't like it.

I refused to be like my mom and cry all the time. I would be perfectly fine if they all would just leave me alone! I hoped nobody around our new house found out my dad was dead.

Every week, Mom made us go to this new church. She said, "Church is a good place to meet people. Our family needs support from other Christians and help to understand God's plan for us. They'll help us learn about God's love and how He can support us through this terrible time."

"But I'm fine! I don't need any help! Especially from God! What did He do to help Dad?" I pushed my little brother away from touching me. "Why can't everyone just leave me alone?"

Mom looked back at me. "You need to start dealing with your anger, Max."

"What anger? I'm not mad anymore!" As I walked into church, I glared at her and then went to my class.

One good thing at church was I had a really great Sunday school class and a cool teacher named Ms. Elizabeth. We played games, listened to music, and learned about the Bible in fun ways. One week, Ms. E asked us if it was okay to get mad.

We all yelled, "No way!"

A boy named Sam said what we all were thinking; "I always get into trouble if I get mad."

Ms. Elizabeth asked, "Does God get angry?"

Mia raised her hand and blurted out, "God can't get angry, He's God."

Then Ms. E divided us into groups and gave us scriptures to look up. Our group found the verse in 2nd Chronicles 24:18. Sarah read it to everyone. "These things made the Lord angry."

Each group read their verses. It amazed me how much God talked about being angry. Jake's scripture, Mark 15:11, even told about how Jesus got mad when he turned over tables at those guys selling stuff in his Father's house.

I didn't understand. If God got angry, why couldn't I? Ms. E said that the next week, we'd learn what God did when He got angry. I couldn't wait to hear. I wondered what kind of stuff God could do when he was upset.

The next week in class, we were all excited to learn what God did when He got mad. All I could think about was if I did what God did, then I couldn't get in trouble anymore. First, Ms. Elizabeth had us all yell out things that made us mad.

Everyone was saying dumb stuff that didn't seem to matter. I wanted to say "my dad committed suicide," but I didn't.

"Now listen, boys and girls, when God got angry, the Bible talks about at least two different things He did. The first was not to keep the anger inside. Let's all read Psalms 103:8 together. Ready?"

"He will not keep his anger forever."

"Secondly, God stayed calm, even though he was mad. Let's read Ecclesiastes 7:9."

"Keep your anger under control; it is foolish to hold a grudge."

"See, children? God understands when we are angry, but He doesn't want us to be angry forever. He wants us to forgive others like He forgives us. And it's very important to get rid of our anger in a way that doesn't hurt anyone."

She gave us a project that week to find the best way to get rid of our anger and then to think of someone we needed to forgive.

For the anger of man does not produce the righteousness of God.

James 1:20

Let all bitterness and anger...be put away from you.

Ephesians 4:31

He that is slow to anger is better than the mighty.

Proverbs 16:32

1) little sister bothers m
2) parents said no to new bibycle
3) friend didn't invite m
   ting
   brand new Game Boy
   broke
5) had to help mom clea

I was determined to find the best way to get rid of anger in a good way. I asked my aunt what she did when she was upset. She said sometimes, she wrote down her feelings in a journal. That was probably a good idea, but sounded too much like homework and not a lot of fun.

My counselor told my mom to get us a punching bag. That was kind of fun, but then my brothers would want to hit it right when I was. I didn't like that.

One afternoon, my uncle filled up five hundred water balloons, and I threw them at his house. It made me feel a lot better and boy was that fun. I couldn't wait to take all the busted balloons in to show everyone. I would win for sure.

After throwing the balloons, I thought about how Ms. E wanted us to find someone to forgive. Almost all the grown-ups told me that I had a lot of anger in me, and they were probably right. But I really didn't know exactly what really made me mad.

I got sick to my stomach if I thought about my dad committing suicide. I'd want to throw up. I couldn't even bear thinking about it. So I guess I hated my dad for dying the way he did.

I didn't understand why my dad would do something like that. I missed him so much, and I wanted things back the way they were before he got sick. I remember when my dad was happy. How did his depression get so bad that he wanted to die? How could I forgive him for leaving me?

I trust in your mercy; my heart rejoices in your salvation
Psalms 13:5

...they shall have everlasting joy, and sorrow shall flee away.
Isaiah 35:10

I will comfort them and make them rejoice from their sorrow.
Jeremiah 31:13

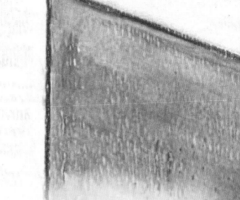

A couple months later in Sunday school, Ms. Elizabeth talked about sadness. She must have figured out I was having a bad day listening to everyone whine about dumb stuff, because she asked my mom if I could stay with her instead of going to the service.

When it was just the two of us, we talked about how sad my dad was from his depression. She told me that in the Bible, God talks about people like my dad who were so sad they wanted to die.

One was a man named Job. He had lots of problems and had a hard time dealing with all of them. Really bad things kept happening to him until he wanted to die, too, like my dad. She showed me Job 7:16 in the Bible where Job said, "I give up; I am tired of living." I guess that's how my dad felt.

Another man who had a hard time was Jonah. He got thrown into the ocean and swallowed by a whale. Ms. Elizabeth read me Jonah 4:3, after the whale swallowed him. It said he prayed, 'Lord let me die! I'd be better off dead than alive.'

She said, "Jonah was having a lot of troubles and he wanted to die. But instead of hurting himself, he prayed. God told him what to do and he listened. He trusted the Lord to help him through that horrible time, and God did. He never gave up on God's plan for him and after that, he always did what God wanted him to."

I will comfort them and make them rejoice from their sorrow.
Jeremiah 31:13

Ms E. hugged me tight. "Max, what happened to you was horrible. And most likely, other terrible things will happen to you in your life. But always remember, God will never leave you."

She opened her Bible to Hebrews 13:5 and read it. "For He Himself hath said, I will never leave thee or forsake thee." She lifted my chin. "Do you understand, Max? God will never, ever leave us. He promises. If anyone ever feels as sad and alone as your dad did, if he'll only ask, God will be with him and comfort him and give him strength."

She handed me a rock. Engraved in the rock was a scripture, 'For the joy of the Lord is your strength. Nehemiah 8:10'

Over the next few months, I decided to learn more about God's words and how He could help me. I actually read some of the Bible and talked with my family and people at church. Everyone said God would give me strength, but how? I didn't understand.

One day, I walked to Grandma's house. I found her on the couch reading her Bible. I cuddled next to her. "How does God give us strength, Grandma?"

She licked her finger and started thumbing through the pages. "Here it is, right here in Matthew Chapter 11, verses 28 and 29, 'Come to me...I will give you rest. Take my yoke and learn from me'."

I looked up and her snowy hair reminded me of a halo. "So, what? God has an egg? I have to crack it to get the yolk and it'll make me smart?"

She laughed. "No, my love, a yoke is a piece of wood strapped across the necks of two oxen. It helps them work together to pull a heavy load that they might not be able to pull by themselves. We must stay close to God, not turn our backs to Him. He says, 'Come to me.'"

"But how can we? Go to Him, I mean."

"Simple. We pray." She put her hand over my heart. "God is always here. With you, Max. Helping you carry your heavy burden, your pain. He's on one side of the yoke and you're on the other. He is carrying it with you."

"Max, you have to trust what the Lord tells you to do, and do it."

"But I never hear Him."

"Not with your ears like you hear my words, but listen with your spirit when you pray, and you'll hear His words in your mind. He will talk to you through His words in the Bible, too. Inside the Bible and within prayer, that's where He gives you strength. You can't have strength without God's word and prayer."

When I went to bed that night, I got on my knees and prayed.

"God, thank You for always being with me. Please help me understand what happened to my Dad, why his depression made him so miserable. I know he believed in You and Jesus. I wished he would have read Your Bible more and asked You for help with his depression.

"Thank You for finding me and reaching out to me, God. For bringing me Ms. Elizabeth to teach me about my Dad's sadness and how You understood. Lord, please keep giving me strength and most importantly help me to forgive."

I cried that night for the first time since Dad died.

I felt like someone was holding me.

I'm pretty sure it was God.

It took me a long time to learn that what my dad did was wrong, and that it wasn't anyone's fault. God did not want him to end his life; God wanted him to live. But God is so good to forgive us when we do wrong.

I found in the Bible where there's no such thing as good and bad sins. They're all the same and they all separate us from God. But if we repent and ask Him to forgive us, He does.

Because God is so good to forgive us, I know I will one day see my dad again in Heaven. The Bible says, "God treats everyone alike. He accepts people only because they have faith in Jesus Christ. All of us have sinned and fallen short of God's glory. But God treats us much better than we deserve, and because of Christ Jesus, he freely accepts us and sets us free from our sins." (Romans 3: 22-24)

That's faith. Believing in Jesus Christ and confessing our sin lets us be in God's presence.

If my dad asked, I know God forgave him. The Bible tells me in Luke 6:37 'Judge not, and ye shall not be judged...forgive, and ye shall be forgiven'. So I have to. I've tried really hard to forgive my dad; I had to ask God for help. It's taking me a lot longer to forgive him than it took God.

I don't know why my dad killed himself or why his depression got so bad, why he didn't get help from the right doctors. I don't know why he thought suicide was his only choice. Only God knows.

But I do know my dad loved me very much, and he didn't want to hurt me. I know I didn't do anything to cause my dad to kill himself. There wasn't anything I could have done to save him either.

I never want to feel like my dad did, and I never want to hurt the people I love as much as my dad hurt me and my family.

I will have faith in God, and He will give me strength. I will pray to Him and stay close to Him. Jesus said He will give me His joy. Everyday, if I try to get closer and know Him better, I'll get more and more of His happiness and love.

My hurt will go away. I liked it when the Bible said He will turn my tears into laughter. I want to read my Bible and pray and be as close to Him as I can. I want to tell everyone how wonderful God is.

'... ye shall be sorrowful, but your sorrow shall be turned into joy.'
John 16:20

Max, (Readers, start with your own name here as you read this scripture.)

'Why then do you complain that the Lord doesn't know your troubles or care if you suffer injustice? Don't you know? Haven't you heard? The Lord is the everlasting God; He created all the world. He never grows tired or weary. No one understands His thoughts. He strengthens those who are weak and tired. Even those who are young grow weak; young men can fall exhausted.' Isaiah 40:27-30

'But those who trust in the Lord for help will find their strength renewed. They will rise on wings like eagles; they will run and not get weary; they will walk and not grow weak.' Isaiah 40:31

Heavenly Father,

Thank You for sending Your Son and making a way for me to be with You forever. I know I have done wrong, and I'm sorry. I understand that when Jesus died on the cross, He made it possible for me to be forgiven, so please forgive me and save me now. I want You to be the Lord of my life and live in my heart.

In the Name of Jesus, Amen.

'For God so loved the world that He gave His only begotten Son that whosoever believed in Him would not perish but have everlasting life.'

John 3:16

*** verses taken from the Good News Bible -Today's English Version; the New American Standard and the King James version.

For more information for children grieving a loved one's suicide please go to:

www.InTheWakeOfSuicide.com